VRM3 FILES

Episode 1

Dexter Alvaro

Thank you, Leic, for your love and support,
Ziah for teaching me patience,
Zeke for making me laugh,
and Amelie for your insight.

Reality is perception. For real!

We all live in a world full of love and hate, hope and despair, real and virtual. So, it only makes sense to choose the right one that feels real to us, even if we have to fake it to transform negativity into positivity.

I get hate for reasons I have no control over. Believe me when I say that it is indeed real and not perceived. I should know, I have endured the scrutiny of my peers and some parents for three years.

Since the beginning of my freshman year, when four freshman moms disappeared with my father, that's when I learned how to be comfortable with a solitary life. It's like high school is my jail, and I've been in solitary confinement. This year is my last, and I can't wait to receive my get out of jail card (HS diploma).

Do you want to hear the rumors about why my dad disappeared?

This school year's most popular rumor is that my father was an arms dealer, and he used the four moms as leverage to seal the deal. Coming in second by a nose, and happened to be the most popular long-running narrative, my father was a religious cult leader who sacrificed himself and the moms. And by far, the silliest thing of all was that he's currently living with four women. I say it's ridiculous because I know for sure that my parents argued a lot; if he had difficulty living with his wife, then how in the world can he survive with four women. I mean, I wouldn't dare consider living with four women, why would he.

Plus, it's hard to fathom why the women liked my father. He was a skinny, nerdy British man who loved observing people rather than communicating with them.

The truth is, I miss people watching with my father. I loved doing that with him. He taught me how to be perceptive and how to read people. When I was younger, I thought he was a detective or even a spy. And when I was in fifth grade, he attended a school event and introduced himself and what he did for a living; I realized I was wrong and agitated that he's not MI6. He was a video game developer who studied people and infused his knowledge into his profession.

My mother often tells me that she envies my relationship with my father because he communicated to me more than her. She told me stories of how she pursued him relentlessly. She recently admitted that she had to marry my father or go back to the Philippines. Her work visa was about to expire, and she did her best to make my father fall for her. She was not proud to admit this. But, since their relationship resulted in making me, then it wasn't for naught after all. She proudly states that her best work is me since I look like a teenage Nicole Scherzinger.

I recently watched 'The Sixth Sense' with my mom. I caught feelings when I watched this because my dad and I watched it together three years ago, before his untimely disappearance. That's probably the last time we spent time together. It's ironic how I wish I could be like that kid who could talk to dead people. Well, I'm not sure if dad's still alive; he sure ghosted us, though.

◆ ◆ ◆

Ever since my father disappeared, my mother and I drew closer. We've been besties for the last three years. Well, not the traditional BFF like shopping together and buying matching outfits. Or even going on a vacay somewhere or a night or two of staycation here in NorCal. We don't even call each other.

Anyway, lately, we haven't seen much of each other. She claims that she's way too busy because of work. I think she's taking advantage of the opportunity of being single. I feel for her, especially when my grandma (mother's side) visits us. Nana Pia often blames my mom for not pursuing a medical career or becoming a nurse. She would often say, "If you were a nurse, you don't need to finesse a posh man for a four-carat diamond ring. Instead, you are a hopeless single woman stuck in that stupid dating thing."

Whenever my mom's home, I get on her case for being on her phone too much. She spends 50% of her time on that popular dating app, 25% on a pic & vid sharing app, 25% on online shopping apps. And, yes, I know that for sure because I frequently monitor her Screen Time.

Okay, I get it. I don't sound like your regular phone-slave, social-media-fiend teenage kid. Don't judge me.

Yes, I do have a phone. But it's not my world. I am not attached to it. And, yes, I have a "Prompt" account.

To the uninitiated, Prompt is the go-to social media for teenagers. A Prompt user can micro-blog, share pics or vids, DM, or chat. The adults shun this fantastic mobile app, so the kids gobble it up since they are oblivious of this innovation.

Prompters (users) keep their lives secrets to their parents or guardians through this app. I, on the other hand, don't keep secrets from my mom. I'm an open book. It's too bad she doesn't have the time to read. Oh, well. Back to the topic at hand.

According to the latest article I read about Prompt, there are 10 million active users. About 99% of Prompters have double or triple-digit numbers of squires, otherwise known as connections. These individuals use the platform as a communication tool.

An average of 100,000 Prompters worldwide receive college scholarships or investment opportunities because they have several thousand squires. Personal branding is the goal of being on the platform.

But only about 100 out of 10 million active Prompters are Pms, Prompters with million squires. Pms are not influencers that enrich themselves; instead, they utilize the platform to enact social change and improve others' lives.

High school kids in the US use Prompt as a branding platform to catapult their career or fast-track their admission to a reputable university. Nowadays, kids are woke, and they don't want debt to hold them down.

It's a gift from the social media gods if you know how to brand yourself. On the flip side, it's a curse if somebody clowns you, and it goes viral. If and when that happens, you better have an army of squires to battle with or for you. But if you have a two-digit squire count, consider yourself canceled.

Are you a perceptive person? Do you want to play a game? Please say, "Yes." Indulge me. Cool.

Let me give you some clues. I am Aidan Peet, a senior at South City Tech - a private satellite STEAM school in Northern California. I love music, and I'm into sports. I have leadership qualities and kind of a big deal. Oh, and I'm biracial.

Let's play, "Where's Aidan?" Ready?

Allow me to set the stage.

South City Tech, fondly referred to as SCT, is a prep school to tech-focused universities. Our campus is a tall glass building. There are rumors that a tech company that went bankrupt donated this building as a form of good faith to South City local officials. Nobody knows the truth. We all subscribe to the notion that it's a friendly, generous ghost from parts unknown.

SCT is dubbed the pre-internship to big tech by Wired magazine. My dad once told me that a tall guy with decent shooting skills has a better chance in the NBA than being admitted to SCT. Our school prides itself on diversity but requires students to wear uniforms; girls and boys wear grey polo shirts and blue jeans because equality is key. Admission is by invite only. So, when a student drops out, the news is broadcasted on social media immediately. And the draft lottery begins. But, enough about my alma mater.

Time to find Aidan. It's lunchtime. Find me in the cafeteria by following the aroma of high hopes, gluten-free tuna melt, knock-off French perfume & cologne emanating in a well-lit, high-ceiling open-space room. I am amongst the teenagers who park themselves around Yin and yang design round plastic tables. It may be a tall task since teenagers flock according to their DNA, personal affinity, drip, and flex status.

Zoom in to the middle of the cafeteria, and you'll find the four royalties of SCT. It's odd to think that they are the nucleus of SCT's society because their career goals don't align with our school's mission statement.

A six-foot-three, skinny, and pasty teenage boy holds court in a table full of really tall bros with fire sneakers. He scrolls through his phone, smiles, and says, "Yo, bruh. Check it out. Tyler Herro liked my post, man. I'mma get drafted after High School. Just watch." Could that be Aidan? Naw. That's Earl Kincaid (Caucasian & Korean). He's SCT's varsity boys basketball's starting shooting guard and team captain. Earl has 25,000+ squires and uses *Kid_E@r1* on Prompt. IMHO, Earl should focus on improving his defense instead of being an NBA Stan.

A five-foot-ten teenage boy with funky dreads dominates a table of boys and girls with dope hairstyles. He holds his phone, bobs his head while music blasts through a Bluetooth speaker. He raps in sync with ROCKSTAR's song (by DaBaby & Roddy Ricch), "We spin his block, got the rebound, Dennis Rodman / You fool me one time, you can't cross me again." He stops the song and says, "Aye, beats straight fire. No offense, bars' lame tho. Facts." Is that Aidan? Nah. He's Jair Ohno-Maia (Brazilian & Japanese). But he goes by *@1r_J* on Prompt, and he has 10,000+ squires. I think he could have more squires if he creates content instead of being a rap critic.

Opposite Earl's table is where the leaders of tomorrow congregate. The kids in this table constantly flex their mental muscles; their leader, a five-foot-six boy wearing a tweed jacket, fiddles with his phone. He gets up, clears his throat, says, "I checked the ROI on fundraisers, and the verdict is: Royal_Tea_Time drinks. We'll flood SCT with tea for maximum profitability." This has to be Aidan, right? Nope. He's Dakshi Yang (Chinese & Indian). Dakshi's Prompt name is *D_Y@ng1*. I think he's teetering on 1,000+ squires. Don't let his stature and low squire count fool you. He makes up for his big ideas.

The table surrounded by a herd of teenagers belongs to SCT's queen. A five-foot-eleven teenage girl with a perfect jawline structure sits by herself while she snaps a selfie. She shows the fresh pic to her literal squires, "Straight fire. Go and fire-up Prompt's algo." This has to be Aidan, right? Wrong. This is Laira Salamanca-Spellman (Caucasian & Mexican). She is SCT's Senior class president and has the most squires in our school. She has 100,000+ squires. You could check out her Prompt pics and vids at *Magic@l_1.*

If you're perceptive, then you discern that SCT's popular kids' high squire count is closely related to how their clout swings the pendulum to their desired outcome. But, I'm getting ahead of myself. Let's not worry about that for now.

Where's Aidan?

Do you see the organically tanned kid with shoulder-length brown hair? She wears a headphone while she sits alone near the exit doors.

She unknowingly raps out loud and out of sync DJ Khaled's & Drake's song (POPSTAR), "I'm a pop star, not a doctor, watch her / Say she rep a whole different block, so I blocked her / Busy at the crib, cookin' salmon with the lobster / If we talkin' joints, it's just me and David Foster."

Yes, that's me. Congratulations. Thanks for playing "Where's Aidan?".

I'm glad you found me. You know what? I always felt like a ghost in this school. But today's different. You see, I didn't realize that I was rapping out loud until I heard a chorus of giggling and laughter. I looked up, and I saw my peers taking a video of my mumbling performance.

Jair raps, "Not a pop star, you Casper, Lil girl / Cali dreamin' Hidden Hills, no sir, not a Jenner / Back to ya crib, find yo missin' father / Leave spittin' lyrics to me and Jacques Berman Webster."

Teenagers erupt in laughter. Earl hollers, "Jair, one. Unknown girl, zero. Hashtag How-2-body-a-cult-kid."

Dakshi adds, "Goodbye. Nice to have not known you."

Laira utters, "Fire-up Prompt's algo. Free cremation."

Jair raps, "Look on bright side tho, my girl / More time to sell tea, yo, Lil girl / To fund search party, find ya poppy / We gon' miss ya, missy, nah, not really."

A student sings a line of Juice WRLD's song (Wishing Well), "This can't be real, is it fiction?".

In a crescendo, the kids' join in unison, "Somethin' feels broke, need to fix it / I cry out for help, do they listen? / I'mma be alone until it's finished."

I stare at my peers, and I can feel lava coursing through my veins. In the blink of an eye, I erupt like a seventeen-year-old dormant volcano, "You all suck! This school sucks! You and SCT can go to Pluto for all I care! You don't exist to me!"

There goes the plot twist to my story. You see, I didn't lie to you. I love music: Hip-Hop, Rap, even Pop. And, I consider myself a hooper Stan because of my dad. Ever since my dad ghosted us, I have been my mom's rock. And, yes, I am a big deal: I'll be the first SCT student to be canceled, virtually & IRL.

A room filled with Psychology, self-help, and "For Dummies" books in the bookcase and wall frames with inspiring quotes:

> "Push yourself, because no one else is going to do it for you."

> "It's okay to be a glow stick. Sometimes we have to break before we shine."

> "If you're offered a seat on a rocket ship, don't ask what seat! Just get on."

A rectangular marble desk nameplate: "Karen LeBlanc | Guidance Counselor" and a MacBook Pro rests in the middle of an ergonomic glass table. Eichler-inspired office furniture adorns the room.

The room screams, "Judge me not, I know I'm pretentious."

Karen LeBlanc, mid-40s, glows as the LED ceiling lights beam on her perfectly made-up face. She could pass for Adele's long lost twin sister - a decade older and the curvier version.

Karen fiddles with a smartphone. She opens an app called "Prompt." She taps on 'Trending,' and the top of the list is **#CAN-CELaidanpeet**, and selects a vid post.

On the video: Aidan explodes, "You all suck! This school sucks! You and SCT can go to Pluto for all I care! You don't exist to me!"

Karen's mouth is agape and green eyes widen as an owl would after spotting its next meal; shocked is an understatement. She's shaking her head as she hands the phone to Aidan.

"Wow! I can't believe you're trending, Aidan. And not in a good way. It's gonna suck. Big time. Take it from me. I've been called Ms. Pounds. Ms. Line Backer. I don't even go on social media anymore ever since that Karen-thing became a thing."

I sigh, "My life's over, Ms. L."

Ms. L playfully taps me on my knee, "Right you are, girl. Hash-tag Terror Thursday. The Internet's brutal. High school kids are a close second. Power through. You'll survive."

My guidance counselor is right. If she endures her cancel-culture monicker, I'm sure it wouldn't be that bad for me.

"What happened, Aidan? Why didya snap?"

I shrug my shoulders, "I dunno. I was just; ya know...minding my business during lunchtime. I was blasting DJ Khaled's POPSTAR on my headphones. But, I didn't realize I was rapping out loud. Kids kept mocking me. Bam! I snapped."

She smiles from ear to ear, "Ooh! That's my jam. I blast that on my way to work, girl. We the best music!"

I smile back, "Isn't Drake the best rapper?"

She frowns and shakes her head, "Nah, girl. Tupac is."

"But you like Drake, right?"

"Well, dude dated Rihanna, so I guess, he aight in my book."

"And the Kardashian & Jenner clan, The Weeknd's girl, Ros Gold-

Onwude, J-Lo, and Bieber's wifey," I add.

She scrunches her nose and shoots me a suspicious look like I sneakily attacked her with a silent stinky fart.

"Why you know so much stuff 'bout Drake's dating life, huh Aidan?" she inquires.

I break a nervous smile, "Well, I got a lot of time on my hands, I guess. You know, the Internet is a wormhole, right?"

She narrows her eyes and asks, "Don't you still work at Royal_Tea_Time?"

I nod, "After school and on the weekend. And since I'm getting canceled. I think I might as well work there full-time until I could get a better gig at the mall."

She pops up and admonishes, "You are not quitting school. Not on my watch."

I get up and say, "And just like Castle Black, them SCT white walkers breached my wall."

She giggles, "Haha, GOT that reference. I know this is your last season, and it sucks," then tap me on my shoulder and says, "life's a long game. It's not about how fast you run; instead, it's about crossing the finishing line. You ain't a quitter, Arya?"

I swallow hard, and my voice shakes as I muster the courage to speak my truth, "I can either stay lo-key and mind my own business until I graduate. Or get bullied on Prompt and in real life. I've stayed off the radar for three years, and I don't think I still have that luxury."

She breaks a nervous smile and caresses my shoulder, non-verbally telling me it's going to be all right.

I take a deep breath and rap a two-liner, "I should just sell tea drinks, spend more time with my momma / instead of dealing with bullies, deflecting my pain and trauma."

Karen gives me a love tap on my upper arm, "You've got bars, girl. Props to Zen."

I chuckle and say, "Haha. I got it from my momma. Whatever. You're only," she shoots me a Kobe-like death stare, "nah, Ms. L. You can't be serious."

"I'm serious, Aidan. Like a Tupac Stan ready to exchange blows with a Biggie fan."

I scrunch my face, "You don't like Biggie?"

She shakes her head and replies, "West Siiiide!"

I burst out laughing, "You loony, Ms. L."

She sings a verse of Taylor Swift's song ME!, "Girl, there ain't no I in 'team' / But you know there is a 'me' / And you can't spell 'awesome' without 'me' / I promise that you'll never find another like."

Somehow, someway, Ms. L minimizes the sting. I smile at her and say, "I appreciate you, Ms. L."

"Anytime, sweetheart. Call or text me. You know how I despise social media."

I don't want to burst my happy bubble right now. I know Ms. L's one of my squires. I mean, no teen will ever use *Real_K@ren* as their Prompt username.

◆ ◆ ◆

The room's vibe is similar to Ms. L, slightly more prominent. Moreover, the bookshelves' books are an eclectic mixture of Psychology, Economics, Technology-related, Basketball-related, and a collection of comic books.

Inspiring wall frame quotes:

"Be a GAME CHANGER the world is already full of players."

"Don't limit your challenges. Challenge your limits."

"You miss 100% of the shots you don't take."

An eclectic array of online college diplomas and certificates is arranged like ladder steps and on the top — 'Honorary Doctorate in Arts and Humanities' from Reale University.

A marble nameplate is twice the size of Ms. L's; it states, "Dr. Michel Maia | SCT Principal."

SCT's principal, Dr. M, but behind his back, others refer to him as McDouble or Michelin. In his late 40s, he's a bit chubby and wears tight-fitting clothes that unsightly bulges of fat give him a semblance of the 'Michelin man' mascot.

Ms. L crosses her arms as she sits across Dr. M. He stares at Ms. L like a hungry bear fresh from hibernation.

"Just admit it, Michel. You told your kid that Dan ran off with your wife, didn't ya?" she proclaims.

He scoffs, "You nuts, woman? Why would I do that? Jair already hates me. I don't need to taint his brain with rumors of Dan's cult."

"He wasn't a cult leader. How many times do I have to tell you? We went on a gaming retreat sponsored by Verme. But, somehow, Dan disappeared with some sketchy Europeans posing as gamers. Nobody knew that they were arms dealers. They tricked Dan into believing they were good guys," she explains.

His voice breaks, "Then why are you here, when my wife is missing?"

She gulps, "I snuck out of the hotel with Trez. I got needs, too, you know. I am sorry your wife is missing. Aidan's dad is missing, three other kids' moms are also missing, and that's the truth. Don't let Jair and his friends bully an innocent girl."

He shakes his head, "Don't be a Karen, LeBlanc!"

She shoots him a death stare, "Talk to your son, Michel!"

He brings his palms up near his chest like he's doing air push-ups, "Chill, woman. You know I can't do that. Jair's not gonna do what I tell him. Quit involving yourself in these kids' dramas."

She gets up, wags her pointer finger, "That's the reason why kids never reach out to you. You never treat them with respect. It also wouldn't hurt if you know how to speak their language."

He pops up. It's a finger-pointing shootout; he wags his chubby pointer finger as he admonishes her, "First, you know I don't speak 'kids.' Second, you and kids nowadays expect respect like it's in demand. I ain't gonna budge and flood the market with it, they'll be an oversupply, and it'll never reach equilibrium. You know that!"

She stares at his wall of accolades, "Whatever, McDouble," gestures at one of Michel's online college certificates on the wall, "Minor in Economics," picks up a book from the bookshelf, "reading Freakonomics."

Michel says, "Ooh, you gotta check out their podcast. Dubner is lit."

She shakes her head, "Whatever, dude. It doesn't make you an economist. Just a poser. Like father, like son."

He huffs and puffs, and wags his finger intensely as he got electrocuted. She extends her right arm with fist clenched then abruptly opens it. Boom! Mic drop moment.

R oyal_Tea_Time is a beverage chain store that offers bubble teas, milk teas, smoothies. Their logo is a gender-neutral character wearing golden wayfarer sunglasses and a golden tea leaf crown. Globally known female Pop, R&B, Hip-Hop, Rap artists adorn the walls. RT2 is a popular hangout place for teenagers since SCT students receive discounts on their drinks, and it offers a frequent-buyer card (golden-card), which allows a free drink after a purchase of $25. The best, though, is if you work here, the owner pays double the minimum wage. How awesome is that? I wonder if the owner even cares if she makes a profit or breaks even.

The store is closing. I'm mopping the floor.

RT2 owner/manager, Maxima Chiu, mid-40s, approaches me and taps my shoulder, "I'm ready to chat now, Aidan." She sits down.

I rest the mop on the wall and sit next to Ms. Chiu. My heart skips a beat as I find the right words to convey without beating around the bush, "I was, you know, hoping if it's okay with you, Ms. Chiu," I clear my throat, not sure if its nerves or dry mouth, "I would like to work full-time."

Ms. Chiu's gentle eyes widen, "Is everything okay?"

OMG, she reads me like an open book. Should I tell her the truth? I look around, avoiding eye contact, "You mean about working here?"

She shoots me an expressionless face like that straight face emoji. Is she genuinely concerned about my well being? I shoot her a nervous smile and wait for her to respond, but her poker face tells me that she's eager for me to spill the tea.

I sigh, "It's school. I snapped, said things I didn't really mean, and now the kids wanna cancel me."

She shakes her head, "Oh, Aidan. I'm sorry. Cancel culture is a deadly virus."

I can't believe she understands what I'm going through. I add, "Do you know if there's a vaccine available?"

Ms. Chiu giggles, "Aw, Aidan, dear, you're funny." She caresses my hand, "Don't quit SCT. Quitting is for losers, sweet-tea. You're a winner, aren't you?"

I look at her straight in the eyes and say, "I'm a dub, Ms. Chiu."

I pop up and grab the mop. As I continue to clean the sticky mess on the floor, I can't help but think that perhaps Ms. Chiu knows something about my dirt on social media.

Ms. Chiu is wiping the tables. I approach her and ask, "Have you seen the Prompt vid yet?"

She grins and says, "Teenagers keep this business afloat. Of course, I saw the video."

My eyes almost pop-out of its sockets, "Really? Who showed it to you?"

Ms. Chiu avoids eye contact and replies, "Um, you know, some random kid." She clears her throat, "Don't forget to lock up, 'kay?"

I nod, and she walks away. Why is she leaving so soon? Did I spook her? Is she covering for someone? Perhaps the random kid is a co-worker, or maybe a golden-card-holding-customer. But then again, I notice how nice Ms. Chiu is to Dakshi. Could they be related? Am I too paranoid? Perhaps I am. But I know for sure that I am hungry. I can't wait to go home and tell my mom about my miserable day at school.

My phone vibrates, and I get a text from my mom. It states, "Got a hot date, prepped your dinner plate, if you wanna wait, be back home by 12:08 ;)"

I put away my phone. As much as I want to get mad at her, I think about the three long years that she waited for my father to go back home. She suffered enough. She deserves happiness, too.

But my selfish side tells me, "Your father abandoned you as well. If he's happy somewhere with someone else, and your mother's searching for hers, don't be a sucker and wait for yours."

It's about time I look out for myself. I have to control my narrative. I open Prompt and noticed that **#CANCELaidanpeet** is still trending. Also, my squire count is now triple digits. No way! This can't be happening. My inbox is as much as my follower count.

I open a DM from *Be@tr1x*, and it says: "Do us a favor. Leave SCT. I deserve your spot."

Whatever! Just one hater, I'm going to shake it off.

I read a DM from *1Tess@* and it says: "I'mma get your spot. Just watch!"

I shake my head and murmur, "Of course, they followed me so that they could send me a DM. They don't support me; they want me to quit. Read one more. If it's negative, time to delete Prompt."

I scroll through the DMs and pick the message from *D@_1ien*, and it says: "Do you see what I see?"

Who the heck is Da_lien? Is this who I think it is?

I respond, "Haha. *D@_1ien*? Are you taking the piss, mate?"

After I send the message, I wait for *D@_1ien* to respond. And after a few seconds, I noticed the three ellipses. I murmur to myself, "OMG! Is my father trying to contact me?"

A multi-colored, tricked-out Japanese mini-van with magnetic signage on the side door: "Calvin's Cleaning Crew."

A muscle-bound teddy bear, Calvin Colin Crews, aka Trez, is in his late 40s. He drives his work-hard-play-hard vehicle. Calvin prefers his clientele to address him by his birth certificate name, but the people dear to him refer to him as Trez.

He stares at his girlfriend, Karen, as she takes a big bite of her double cheeseburger.

Karen wipes her mouth, "I'm scared, baby."

Trez's heart skips a beat. He thinks to himself, "Am I gonna be a daddy? OMG!" He gulps. He focuses on the road and locates a perfect parking spot for the impending good or bad news.

As soon as he parks the van, he blinks his eyes repeatedly like a nervous giraffe facing a lioness.

"Is everything okay, baby?" he softly utters.

She pouts, "I might lose my job, Trez."

He exhales and utters, "I was hoping to hear that I'm gonna be a daddy."

She playfully hits his chest, "Don't be silly. You know my contract at school doesn't allow me to be pregnant."

He raises his eyebrow, "Am I the only one who thinks that's a weird clause in your contract?"

She snickers, "Haha. You should be thankful I checked that box in the contract."

"It was optional?" he inquires.

"Of course, Trez. It's unconstitutional to prevent a woman from being pregnant while being gainfully employed," she replies.

He shakes his head, "I don't get it. Why didya sign then?"

She places her burger inside the paper bag. She womansplains to him, "Checking that box means I ain't going to miss work because of maternal leave."

He shrugs his shoulders, "No need to worry then, right?"

She replies with a blank stare.

"Just give me the backstory why you're freaking out about your job security," he says.

She exhales, "One of my kids. She's sweet. Her name is Aidan. She's a senior now."

"Zen and Dan's daughter, right?"

She nods, "Yes. She got bullied on social media today. The kids got her trending in a bad way. They wanna cancel her, baby."

"Cancel? Like get her fired, I mean, kicked-out of school?" he asks.

"Yup. I stuck my neck out and told McDouble to tell his son to do something about it."

He shakes his head, "Nah. It ain't gonna happen. Dude is spineless. He ain't sticking his neck out for nobody. Didn't you say Verme got him the job so he won't sue?" he proclaims.

She brings her head down, "That's why I'm freaking out, Trez. McDouble is taking a risk by using his son to publicly shaming Dan's daughter," she sighs, "I have a feeling Michel told his kid that Dan, quote-unquote cult leader, is the reason why Yayoi's missing. Dan's a good guy. He's the most creative game developer I've ever known. It's just too bad he partnered with those European terrorist groups."

He bites his lower lip and sighs heavily, "It doesn't matter if Dan's a cult leader or a terrorist. Don't agitate Michelin. Quit defending Dan's kid. I need SCT's business. Your school is my only commercial client left."

"What do you want me to do, Trez?"

"Lie! Tell Michel that Yayoi reached out to ya recently. See if he bites on that," he pleads.

Karen brings out her phone, taps her photos icon, taps library, scrolls up to 2016 album, then selects a group picture: Karen on the far left, next to her is a Japanese woman in her mid-40s - Yayoi Ohno-Maia, an Indian woman in her mid-40s - Mishka Yang, in the middle is a British man in his mid-40s - Daniel Peet, a Korean woman in her mid-40s - Bitna Kincaid, and a Mexican woman in her early-40s - Larissa Salamanca-Spellman.

◆ ◆ ◆

I am finally home in our open space, minimalist-style two-bedroom, one-bathroom apartment. The kind of architectural set-up where you enter from the outside and a few steps is the living room, another few steps, and you're in the dining room, and an arms-length away is the kitchen. Not to sound like a spoiled brat, I miss living in a house.

My mom loves this place because of its proximity to my school. She doesn't have to commute since she works from home.

My mother, otherwise known as Zen (short for Zenaida), is a content specialist. It fascinates me to think that she could've been a software developer or programmer, but she's content on curating her clients' stories.

So, we only have a sofa, a couple of folding chairs, a coffee table in the living room. We don't even have a dining set since we eat together in the living room. Mom didn't even bother buying a TV since we watch on our laptops and mobile phones. The bare-bones interior design was due to a lack of financial resources than a choice.

My school BFF and guidance counselor used to rent the other room, but she moved out a few months ago and now lives with her boyfriend, Trez. They live a few doors down the hallway, but since they appear to be in their honeymoon phase, they spend every available time with each other.

I miss having dinner with my mom and Karen in the living room. None of us know how to cook. More often, we share foot-long sandwiches, Chinese take-outs, value meals, instant ramens.

As I stroll toward the kitchen, I notice a top ramen bowl on the counter. That's definitely the dinner my mother prepped for me. She's so considerate and efficient.

I wish Karen were here, so we could share the bowl and laugh about our day. Well, my life's pretty dull; it's her anecdotes that spark conversation and laughter.

I miss Karen living with us. I am in deep need of a human connection right now. Sometimes I wish I had a video game so that I could chat with another human being.

I am feeling restless, and check the time on my phone. It is now 10:08 pm. I have a couple of hours to spend before my mom gets back from her date.

I am pacing back and forth. My mind can't fathom *D@_1ien*'s claim that he is my father. Who in their right mind would do this to me? Why pretend to be my missing father? Why would someone torture me like this? It defies logic.

It has to be a hater trying to lure his or her way inside of my psyche. I can't believe kids nowadays. Worst, though, what if this is a parent trying to manipulate me into spilling my deepest darkest fears and use it against me. I never realized that weird DMs probably bombard the four SCT royalties as well. I guess it's not all glitters and rainbows if you have numerous squires.

On the bright side, however, what if it's my father? I can finally solve the mystery of his disappearance.

The only way to know if this is real is to tackle it head-on. I need to relax my mind. I sit on the sofa as I stare at my phone.

I focus on my Prompt chat with *D@_1ien*:

D@_1ien: Do you see what I see?

A1d@n: Haha. D@_1ien? Are you taking the piss, mate?

D@_1ien: Sooo sorry. It's been a long three years. In my defense, 3 years inside VRM3 is merely 1 month.

A1d@n: Don't play with me, mate. If you are who I think you are, send me a screen-grab of the last movie we saw together.

D@_1ien: I'm inside a virtual world. I can't do that.

A1d@n: Whatever! You obvs are not the person who you claim to be.

D@_1ien: The Sixth Sense.

A1d@n: Lucky guess. Explain the backstory to my name then.

D@_1ien: Your mum's Filipina nickname plus 'n' in my moniker is the origin of your name.

A1d@n: Nope! You're mistaken, mate. Mom tells me that she re-arranged her name minus 'Ze' of course.

D@_1ien: Ask me something only Daniel Peet would know.

A1d@n: What was the worst school day of my Life?

D@_1ien: It's a tie between this afternoon and the time I attended your fifth-grade "Meet-a-parent" event when you expected me to tell your class that I am MI6.

A1d@n: I miss you, dad.

D@_1ien: I can't wait to see you again, luv. I miss you, too. Download the Verme app link: (VRM3) and pair it with my VR goggles. Remember to access the game with your Prompt account; otherwise, your consciousness remains inside the virtual world like me. Tap on the VRM3 app and search D@_1ien, select it, and tap on "Chat Now." Don't forget to place your phone inside your pocket before you wear the VRM3 goggles. See you soon.

I get up and enter my bedroom. I open my closet and search the plastic box container labeled "Debt collectors docs." Inside the container is a black backpack. I open the zipper and pull-out the VR goggles labeled VRM3.

I sit on the edge of my bed.

I download the app link to my mobile phone, and the login access pops up. I click on it and follow my dad's instruction: Access the VRM3 app with my Prompt account. I pair the VRM3 app with the VRM3 goggles and place my phone inside my pocket.

I murmur to myself, "I hope my sixth sense is right."

I wear my dad's VRM3 goggles.

W eirdly, I see an augmented reality version of my father standing in our school's lobby. I can't believe my eyes; it feels like we're Pokemon Go characters. I've dreamt of this day since they informed us about his disappearance. I mean, sure he's like a hologram, his face looks the same, except his body appears to be physically fit.

He runs towards me, gives me a bear hug, and plants a kiss on my cheek.

D@_1ien: Oh, sweetheart. I missed you so much.

My virtual dad's firm grip makes me feel so emotional. He stares at me, and I look away. His virtual blue eyes are too much for me to handle. I wiggle out of his hug. I start to walk, and he follows me.

A1d@n: Why didn't you come back, dad?

He attempts to hold my hand, and I swipe it away.

D@_1ien: I wanted to, luv. But It's not up to me.

I clear my throat and muster the courage to lock eyes with him.

A1d@n: Aren't you the game developer?

He shoots me a smile.

D@_1ien: Yes. But I still answer to Vayn Reale.

I fold my arms.

A1d@n: The VR guy?

At that moment, I realized that I hadn't seen my avatar self. I face a glass wall and stare at my reflection. Wow! The resemblance is uncanny. I think to myself, "I wish I am fit." Instantly, my virtual appearance changes to my desired state. I see my dad's reflection; he's smiling at me.

D@_1ien: He's more than that, sweetheart. Vayn is the reason I can get in touch with you. He's been taking care of you and the others.

I face him.

A1d@n: By 'the others', you mean the kids of the four missing moms, right?
D@_1ien: Yes. How are those kids adjusting?

I walk away, and he follows me.

A1d@n: I don't want to talk about my bullies, dad.

He puts his arm around my shoulders.

D@_1ien: Sorry, luv. I had no idea about your life in the real world. We were so focused on fixing the VRM3 game's virtual problem; we failed to realize that we've been gone for years. Well, our consciousness, at least.
I shoot him a confused look.

A1d@n: What do you mean by that, dad?

He sighs.

D@_1ien: Our physical form is well intact, but it's merely a turtle's shell because our consciousness is in VRM3's virtual world.

I frown.

A1d@n: Why am I here then, dad?

He flashes his pearly whites.

D@_1ien: We are hoping that your presence here will help us figure out what's missing. And when we find out the solution, we can go back to the real world.

◆ ◆ ◆

It blows my mind knowing I am finally communicating with my father, albeit in virtual space. But then again, I don't recall having a phone convo with my mom in the past three years; it's usually through gifs or texts. It is overwhelming to feel real emotions right now.

The weirdest thing is that my father and I sit on the rooftop of the SCT building overlooking NorCal's South City. My palms are so clammy, and it freaks me out how real this feels right now.

My father stares at me, and I could see my reflection through his eyes, magical and haunting at the same time.

D@_1ien: What's on your mind, luv?

I give him an MJ (Michael Jordan) shrug.

A1d@n: Dunno, dad. I'm still kinda lost with the whole thing about you missing for three years.

He looks up to the full moon as if he's channeling the VR god, Vayn Reale, for enlightenment.

D@_1ien: Let me put it in simple terms: spending 1 VRM3 hour equals 3 days in the real world, 1 VRM3 day equals 3 weeks, 1 VRM3 week equals 3 months, 1 VRM3 month equals 3 years.
A1d@n: Lemme see. You've been inside VRM3 for a month, right?

He nods and massages his face as if he's perplexed by the vast disparity of real and virtual time-lapse.

D@_1ien: Indeed, sweetheart. Get your phone, please.

I take out my phone, and the home screen is a digital timer that reads "59:01" with the seconds counting down.

D@_1ien: I am giving you 1 VRM3 hour, which means you'd be missing in the real world for 3 days.

I shoot him a side-eye and pocket my phone.

A1d@n: What?! No way, dad.
D@_1ien: Do you want to stay longer?

I widen my eyes at him.

A1d@n: You nuts?! OMG, dad! Of course, you are. We've missed you for three years, and now that we've finally reconnected, you want my mother to worry about me missing for three days.

He pops up and paces.

D@_1ien: Oh, my dear, Aidan. Don't you worry. She's not going to miss you.

I get up and follow him.

A1d@n: She will miss me, dad. Believe me.

My father stares at a drone-like helicopter flying towards us. The helicopter shines its spotlight at us. I freak out and lie down face to the floor. My father laughs.

D@_1ien: Get up, Aidan.

I get up and stand behind my father. The helicopter descends on the rooftop. In a few seconds, the engine shuts off. The driver-side door opens, and a man in his late 50s steps out. He has a cool soccer-hairstyle, wears a Hawaiian polo shirt, boardshorts, and pastel-mix kicks. He looks like a retired Neymar. He holds a mobile phone as he walks toward us.

I whisper to my dad.

A1d@n: What's going on? Who the heck is that guy? More importantly, can he see us?

My father playfully ruffles my hair.

D@_1ien: To see is to believe, right? Meet the VR god: Vayn Reale. In the flesh.

Vayn keeps his eyes fixed on a mobile phone as he saunters towards us. I wave at Vayn, but he walks right through me.

A1d@n: Over here, Vayn.

I raise my eyebrow at my dad. He taps my shoulder.

D@_1ien: It's okay. This is the first time for everybody.

Vayn turns around and holds the phone like he's about to take a selfie. I stare at the mobile screen, and it appears as if Vayn's using a real-life augmented reality game.

"Bravo, Dan! You and the VRM3 team did it. Who's the lovely

young lady next to you?" Vayn says.

I wave my hand, and Vayn reciprocates.

A1d@n: Hello, Vayn. I am Aidan Peet. Dan's daughter.

As I speak, I could hear my voice because older people like to use the speaker on their phones. Also, I can see the caption pop-up on Vayn's mobile phone. It is inconceivable to witness the real-time transfer of communicative data of the real-world and virtual world.

My father waves his hand and Vayn waves back.

D@_1ien: Hi, Vayn. I think it's time my daughter meets the rest of the VRM3 team.

Vayn smiles, "I think you're right, Dan. Do you know how to do a group chat, Aidan?"

I shoot him a stink eye.

A1d@n: Is Pluto a planet, Mr. Reale?

Vayn giggles and replies, "Ooh! I need Lavender essential oil for that burn; otherwise, it's gonna make a mark. Anyhoo. Get your phone and swipe up to access VRM3. Select the following squires: *B1t_n@, Y@_yo1, M1sh_k@, L@_r1ssa.*"

I bring out my phone and follow his instructions. I tap on the group chat option and select the squires he mentioned.

After clicking the option "Chat Now," the missing freshman moms appear before my virtual eyes. Their pearly whites blind me as they all grin from ear to ear.

B1t_n@: Hello, Aidan. I'm Bitna Kincaid. Earl's mom. Is he pretty good at basketball now?

I smile at the virtual version of Mrs. Kincaid.

A1d@n: He's quite a hooper, Mrs. Kincaid. He's NBA-bound for sure. That is if he works on his defense so that he'd be a two-way player.

My dad smiles at me and adds,

D@_1ien: I miss watching NBA games with you, luv.
Y@_yo1: I'm Yayoi Ohno-Maia. Jair's mom. How's my boy? Is he still into that rap thing? By the way, I heard Michel is SCT's school principal: is he good with the students?
A1d@n: Yes, Mrs. Ohno-Maia. Jair's got bars. Mr. Maia is, you know, doing his best, I think.
M1sh_k@: Hi, Aidan. I'm Dakshi's mom, Mrs. Yang. Is Dakshi small for his age? Are you taller than him? Level with me. I'm not easily offended.

I avoid looking at her piercing brown eyes.

A1d@n: Um...he's probably, uh, still growing, Mrs. Yang. But to answer your question, yes, I am taller than Dakshi.

Dakshi's virtual mom rolls her eyes.

L@_r1ssa: Hello, Aidan. Remember me? Mrs. S. Laira's mom. How close are you two now? I bet you're BFFs like when you're in Middle School.

I swallow hard. As much as I want to divulge the truth to Laira's virtual mom, I don't want to hurt her feelings.

A1d@n: Not as close as we were, Mrs. S, but I'm sure we both are just into our things at the moment.
L@_r1ssa: Aw, sweetie. What happened? Did you have a falling out or something?

I don't know why suddenly I feel the urge to bawl out in front of them. I want the VRM3 team to understand that being MIA resulted in an avalanche of negative emotions on our part.

A1d@n: To be honest, Mrs. S, ever since all of you went missing, all of us suffered. I have been lonely for three years. I don't have a single friend at school.

Vayn sighs and proclaims, "I am sorry to hear that, Aidan. But I assure you that the sacrifice you made is not in vain. Because of your father and the VRM3 team, we can help the government prevent internet crimes. But we're not there yet. By the way, not sure if you are aware of the meaning of Verme or VRM3. The public knows that it stands for Vayn Reale's Mechanical Enterprise, and they also believe that it went bankrupt. And I would like that narrative to stay constant."

A1d@n: You're the friendly, generous ghost who donated our school to South City.

Vayn nods, "Yup, and keep that fact intact, please. Anyhoo, you're currently using a VRM3 program called Virtual Reality Metaverse Experience. I have a contract with InternetPol to beta-test that program. Dan and his team created an AR game wherein the user's life-like holographic image appears in real life and in real-time. But it's not there yet, sooner I hope. I have a person from the real world working hard on that patch. The virtual team, however, is working hard on ironing out the kinks of the AR game. VRM3 and Prompt's algorithm are working seamlessly right now. And, we need you to beta-test its effectiveness."

A1d@n: Why me? I'm not special.

My father pulls me close, and we lock eyes.

D@_1ien: We picked you because you can do it. I've trained you on how to read people. We believe in you.

I look at each one of them with bright eyes and unnerving belief in me, perplexing and flattering.

◆ ◆ ◆

Zen sits on the driver's side of her compact-size hybrid vehicle. She's taller than the average brown-skin queen from the Far East and is evident as she's having a tough time adjusting to the lack of headroom and legroom inside her car.

She holds her phone like she's taking a selfie. Zen's in a video call with Karen, and it appears that Karen's backdrop image is a shower curtain.

Karen is inside her bathroom, and her phone is attached to a selfie stick.

Karen raps her version of Lauren Hill's classic song (Doo Wop - That Thing): "It's been three years since you were looking for your man / The one who vanished and never called you again / 'Member when he told you he was a 'Family Man' / You act like you ain't know him, then bought his lies and / Where to begin, how you think you're really gon' pretend / Like you a content specialist, but an agent with a hit list."

Zen interrupts, "Yo, yo, girl! Are you alone?"

Karen nods.

"What the hell, girl! I told you to keep everything under wraps," exclaims Zen.

Karen rolls her eyes, "You know it's bound to come out, right? Nothing is sacred anymore. There are no secrets in this world."

"Nobody needs to know our secrets," Zen massages her forehead, frustrated, "look, Karen, I know you and Dan go way back, and I need you to keep it hunnid with me, please," she begs.

With a straight face, Karen replies, "I didn't, and would never tell a soul. Aidan doesn't know. Trez is clueless. People at SCT think I was Dan's former admin assistant. Nobody knows the real truth, okay?"

Zen sighs, "Okay, cool. Did you do what I told ya?"

Karen raises her right eyebrow, "Yup! I went to Michelin's office and accused him of using his son to spread rumors about Dan running away with Yayoi."

Zen breaks a nervous smile, "Good," exhales, "and what about the other parents?"

"I've been spinning the rumor that Dan brokered an arms deal with a terrorist group, and that the other moms weren't privy to his secret dealings, and went missing anyway."

Zen bites her lower lip, "No, no, no, Karen. I told you not to make-up other lies. You should stick to our first lie."

Karen shakes her head, "Nope. The cult lie sucks. Do you know what your daughter is dealing with at school?"

"Aidan's not," clears her throat, "let's not discuss," Zen closes her eyes, takes a deep breath.

Karen raises her right eyebrow, "You gotta stop hating on my tactics, girl," clears her throat, "Yo, Zen. Are we good?"

Zen screams, the veins on her forehead are bulging, "So, you think everyone at school should believe that Dan's a terrorist arms dealer that kills a lot of people, rather than a cult leader who sacrificed the four moms," she's panting, "are you cray?!" she exclaims.

"Chill, girl. Relax, all right. I got this," pleads Karen.

Sweat trickles down Zen's face, her lips quivering, "I am not familiar with your MI6 tactics, and I have no choice but to just," wipes her sweat with her shirt, "go with the flow."

A faint knocking on the bathroom door startles Karen. Trez's muffled voice is coming from the hallway, "Not trying to rush ya, babe. But I feel a ninja turtle tryin' to slice its way out of my..."

Karen ends the call. She murmurs to herself, "Oh my god, oh my god. Trez wasn't supposed to be home yet."

◆ ◆ ◆

Vayn waves goodbye as his helicopter flies away.

B1t_n@ approaches my father. She pleads,

B1t_n@: I would like to see how Earl's adjusting. Could I go first, Dan?

My father nods. He looks at me and says,

D@_1ien: Check the timer, luv.

We both check my phone, and the digital timer reads "52:15".

A1d@n: Question: What happens now?
D@_1ien: Go to the VRM3 app and select "Group Chat." Select Kid_E@r1 and B1t_n@, but for Mrs. Kincaid, click on the BCN box on the "Group Chat."
A1d@n: Are we going to be transported to Earl, dad? Ooh, and is BCN like BCC?

He flashes a hearty smile.

D@_1ien: Yes, and yes, sweetheart.
A1d@n: Another question: How do we get back here?
D@_1ien: Swipe-out the "Group Chat" with Earl. Good? Okay, no more questions, please. Let's be wise with our limited time. Remember, Aidan. Ten minutes only, 'kay?

The digital timer reads "50:15".
I follow my father's instruction, and as soon as I click on "Chat Now," *B1t_n@* and I stand inside Kincaid's apartment, in the living room to be specific, right in front of Earl. Oddly, his living ar-

rangement is like ours.

Earl relaxes on the sofa as he scrolls through his Prompt DMs. He clicks on my "Chat Now" message and scoffs, "No way! Aidan wants to chat? Wonder what she wants."

B1t_n@ kneels and plants Earl a kiss on the cheek. I whisper,

A1d@n: Mrs. Kincaid, can Earl see us?

Earl pops up, and with bug eyes, he looks around, "Hello? Did somebody say something?"

B1t_n@ approaches me and pulls me to the kitchen, a few steps away from Earl. She softly utters to my ear,

B1t_n@: Don't say anything. Earl can't see us, but he can hear you. Later, if he chats with you, use your phone to reply. Remember, not a peep.

I whisper to *B1t_n @*'s ear,

A1d@n: How can he hear and not see me? And what if I sneeze or something.
B1t_n@: Firstly, our virtual self doesn't sneeze or get sick. Even if you're ill or dying in real life, your virtual self is oblivious to your current state. One of the kinks we're dealing with right now is that our hologram is invisible unless the recipient has a VRM3 app on their phone, and they can see us similar to how Vayn did earlier. He can hear you because he clicked on the "Chat Now" command. Don't worry. Your dad will fix that bug soon.
A1d@n: So, are we like ghosts that he can hear but not see?

B1t_n@ nods.

"Hey, Earl. You home?" yells Mr. Kincaid as he enters from the front door.

Earl approaches his dad and gives him a dap.

B1t_n@ murmurs,

B1t_n@: Let's walk over there; I want to hear what they're talking about. Plus, I want to see if Chad's a good father.

We both walk over to Earl and Mr. Kincaid.
They both sit on the sofa.
"Did you say something earlier, dad?" inquires Earl.
"Whatchu talkin' 'bout? You good, Earl? You're not on any harmful substance, right?"
Earl gets up and starts flexing, "Come on, pops. You know I need to keep this vessel in tiptop shape. How else am I going to play in the NBA if I mess with that bad stuff?"
Mr. Kincaid shakes his head, "That's cool, my dude. Sit down. I wanna talk to you about the college offers."
Earl declares, "Nah, dad. I told you. I'm going straight to the G-League if I don't get drafted. Plus, I got this DM from T. Herro. He tells me I got game, ya know. I'm about to blow up on Prompter, just watch."
Mr. Kincaid shakes his head, "Social media is a smokescreen, kid. It ain't real, but you've got real skills. Life's not about taking shortcuts, Earl. It's good to have options. Life without options is like playing Russian roulette."
Earl avoids eye contact.

I pull out my phone, and the Digital Timer reads "40:15." I show the phone to *B1t_n@*, and she hugs Earl.
I give *B1t_n@* a few more seconds and swipe out my "Chat Now" thread with Earl.

Zen sits across a teenage boy wearing a hoodie jacket inside her car. She orders, "Take off that stupid hoodie. I wanna see if you're telling the truth."

He replies, "Look, lady. I'm already here, aren't I? You ain't my mother. Stop bossin' me around."

Zen reaches in her glove box and grabs a pepper spray. She points it at him.

The teenage boy obliges, and it's Jair. He swallows hard, "Look, Mrs. Peet. I did what you told me to do."

"Prove it!" she barks.

Jair's hands are shaking. He pants as he searches for his phone.

"Hurry up, Jair! Show me the proof," she exclaims.

He pulls his phone out from his pocket and drops the phone, "Sorry," he picks it up, opens the Prompt app and clicks on **#CAN-CELaidanpeet**, plays the video, and shows it to Zen.

She watches the video and nods, "Cool. Put your phone away now. Wait. Turn it off first."

Jair is shivering as he follows Zen's instruction. His lips quivering, "Could you please put the pepper spray down, Mrs. Peet? You're scaring me."

She snickers and stuffs the pepper spray inside her shirt, "Go away now, lil boy. Your job is done."

Y@_yo1, myself, Jair, and Mr. Maia are among the diverse groups of people inside a fancy Japanese restaurant. I don't know if I've eaten here before, perhaps not. Plus, I would remember if my dad or Karen brought me to a fancy place.

Jair sits across from Mr. Maia.

Jair's phone rests face down on the table next to his untouched bento box. Though it's a Japanese-owned restaurant, it's still in America, hence the bento box.

Mr. Maia wipes his mouth with a table napkin, and his bento box is empty.

Jair's phone pings.

Y@_yo1 sits next to Jair. She caresses Jair's face. Meanwhile, I sit next to Mr. Maia.

I check the digital timer on my phone, and it reads: "33:15". I place my phone on the table with the screen facing up so I could monitor the time.

Mr. Maia asks, "Hey, J. You gonna eat or what?"

"Not hungry, dad. I already told ya earlier, didn't I?" he whines.

"Relax, man. I'm just worried about you. That's all. You haven't touched your food," Mr. Maia retorts.

"Why are we here, dad?"

Mr. Maia sarcastically replies, "Why?! To eat, of course."

Jair raises his voice one-octave higher, "No, dad. This is mom's favorite place, that's why we're here."

A1d@n: Is that right, Mrs. Ohno-Maia?

Y@_yo1 brings her pointer finger to her lips, gesturing for me to be quiet.

A1d@n: It's okay. Jair hasn't clicked my "Chat Now" message. So he can't hear me right now. And by the way, you could talk, they won't be able to listen to you.

Y@_yo1: You sure? By the way, call me Mrs. OM.

I yell from the top of my lungs, and simultaneously the lights from the restaurant flicker.

Y@_yo1: Why must you yell to prove your point. Anyway, did you

make the lights flicker, Aidan?
    A1d@n: I don't know, Mrs. OM. That's weird, right?

Michel rest's his arms on the table with his hands clasped together, "You're right. I brought you here for a reason."
Jair shoots his father an expressionless face like he doesn't care.

A1d@n: I know why they're here, Mrs. OM.
Y@_yo1: Child, be quiet. We're here as spectators. Let the gladiators duke it out.

I giggle, and *Y@_yo1* covers her mouth, feeling embarrassed about laughing at her joke.

A1d@n: You're funny, Mrs. OM. Why isn't Jair funny like you?
Y@_yo1: J's a clown. He's shy at first, but he grows on you. I should know. He's my boy.
A1d@n: Kinda bias, of course, but I'd take your word, Mrs. OM.
Y@_yo1: Did you guys hang out yet?

I shake my head.

A1d@n: Nah, not yet. I don't plan on it anyway, on account of him embarrassing me.
Y@_yo1: J is a sweet boy. I'm sure he had his reasons. Maybe it's peer pressure; I don't know.

Jair picks up his phone. I rush over to hover over Jair and spy on him. Jair opens Prompt, scrolls to his new messages, and he clicks on my chat request. I rush over to *Y@_yo1* and whisper to her,

A1d@n: He clicked "Chat Now," it's on, Mrs. OM.

Jair murmurs to himself, "Dang, dude. I wonder what Aidan wants."

Y@_yo1: I think he's ready to chat. Get your phone.

I pick up my phone, and the digital timer reads: "31:15".
Jair gets up. I whisper to *Y@_yo1*,

A1d@n: Mrs. OM, we've only got one minute left.
Y@_yo1: Oh, man! Really?

"Where you going, J?" asks Mr. Maia.
"I'mma step out for fresh air. Is that cool?"
Mr. Maia nod. We follow Jair as he proceeds to exit the restaurant.
Jair places a call, "Mrs. Peet. I don't know why Aidan messaged
me. I already followed your instructions, even though I knew it
was wrong to embarrass your daughter. Can you guys please leave
me alone?"
He ends the call.

I check out the digital timer, and it's "30:15". I whisper,

A1d@n: It's time to go.

Jair flinches and starts to walk. *Y@_yo1* follows him. Another
rookie faux pas, as I startle Jair.

Y@_yo1 begs,

Y@_yo1: One more minute, please.

I mouth to *Y@_yo1*, "It's time to go." *Y@_yo1* stops to follow
Jair. She shakes her head.
Y@_yo1: Really?! This sucks, dude.

I whisper,

A1d@n: I'm sorry.

I swipe out my "Chat Now" message with Jair.

Karen paces back and forth. Trez sits upright on the sofa while keeping his eyeballs steady on his girlfriend like he's a Wimbledon tennis umpire.

"Tell the truth, Trez. You were eavesdropping, weren't you?"

"Baby, I wasn't. I swear."

Karen says to herself, "I've got to switch it up. Pivot. Change the topic."

Karen halts and sits next to Trez. She bats her eyelashes at him.

"I'm pregnant, Trez."

He laughs out loud.

She slaps his chest, "Don't laugh. I'm serious."

"Naw, bae. You tryin' to change the topic. That's what you tryna do."

"Aha! Got you, liar. You were eavesdropping."

Trez holds Karen's hand and speaks with a BBC English accent, "Didn't have to, luv. I am privy about your mission, really. Moreover, I am aware that MI6 will release you from your assignment if you're ever pregnant. Is that accurate?"

Karen pops up, eyes popped like popcorn kernels fresh from the microwave, "You MI6, too?"

He taps on the sofa, gesturing her to sit, switches back to his American accent, "C'mon, girl, I'mma spill the tea if you sit."

She obliges, "Go ahead. I'm all ears, Trez."

"Well, I've been assigned to InternetPol for a year now after I finished my coding boot camp at the force."

"So, you're a cop, then?"

He nods, "CIHP, California Internet Highway Patrol. ICD, Internet Crimes Division. I helped put a lot of bad people in jail, so the CIA recruited me. I agreed since I know a lot of bad actors are trying to trick kids on Prompt. Like you, for instance, you have an account, but I know you're just trying to monitor Dan's daughter, right?"

She nods, "Oh, I see," squints her eyes and inquires, "so, Verme didn't recruit you directly?"

He squints back, "Vayn Reale Mechanical Enterprise? Why would they hire InternetPols?"

"You're not aware of Vayn Reale Metaverse Enforcers, huh?" she mutters.

◆ ◆ ◆

I t's closing time at RT2.
Dakshi and Ms. Chiu sit next to each other. Dakshi covers his face with his palm, sobs uncontrollably.
Ms. Chiu rubs Dakshi's back, comforting him, "There, there, Dakshi. It's okay, sweetheart. Just let it all out."

I think to myself, "Aha! Dakshi showed the Prompt video to Mrs. Chiu."

M1sh_k@ hugs Dakshi tightly and sobs as well.

I stand next to *M1sh_k@*, and I caress her shoulder, comforting her.

A1d@n: It's okay, Mrs. Yang. Everything's gonna be alright.

M1sh_k@ looks at me,

M1sh_k@: Why is my baby crying, Aidan?

I shrug my shoulder,

A1d@n: Not sure, Mrs. Yang.

Dakshi wipes his tears and hugs Ms. Chiu, "Thank you, Aunt Max. I don't know what I'd do without you."
"It's okay, Dakshi. I know Aaron could be a pain sometimes."
I tap *M1sh_k@.*

A1d@n: Question, Mrs. Yang: Is Ms. Chiu related to Mr. Yang?

M1sh_k@ nods.

M1sh_k@: Yes. Aaron and Max have the same mother. We just found out about three years ago.
A1d@n: Really? What's the story behind that?
M1sh_k@: Max sold her startup for nearly a quarter of a billion dollars. She was a guest on a popular business-related podcast and mentioned that she inherited her late mother's business acumen.
A1d@n: How did your husband find-out that they are related?
M1sh_k@: The host asked her if she has any kids to pass her business-savvy secrets to, and she replied, "My nephew - Dakshi Yang."
A1d@n: No way. For real?

Dakshi's voice breaks as he asks, "Aunt Max, why do you think my father hates me?"
"Oh, sweetie. Aaron doesn't hate you. I know that for sure. Me, on the other hand, though, I know he hates."
"Is it because of the money you gave me?"
Ms. Chiu shrugs, "Maybe. I don't know. Anyway. Why do you think your father hates you?"
Dakshi replies, "I told dad that I am taking a break after high school to travel to Asia. But he thinks it's a bad idea."

M1sh_k @'s gesturing like she wants to choke Ms. Chiu.

A1d@n: You okay, Mrs. Yang?

M1sh_k@ covers her face with her palms then sighs,

M1sh_k@: Sorry, you had to see that. I can't help it sometimes. I'm not too fond of when she rubs her success on our face like that.

Ms. Chiu caresses Dakshi's hand, "Did you tell your father I gave you the money for your backpacking trip to Asia?"
Dakshi avoids eye contact, "Um...did you want me to lie to him, Aunt Max?"

M1sh_k@ swings wildly at Ms. Chiu, and I grab her from behind, and we both fall. I'm unaware that my virtual self was super intense. We look at each other and laugh.

M1sh_k@: I'm not a violent person, Aidan. I just have a lot of repressed emotions.

I smile at *M1sh_k@,*

A1d@n: It sounds weird, but I understand you, Mrs. Yang.

Ms. Chiu ruffles Dakshi's hair, "I know your parents resented the fact that I was more successful than them. But it's just money," repeatedly blinks to stop the tears from flowing down her cheeks, "they're the ones who are lucky."
Dakshi rubs Ms. Chiu's shoulder, "What makes you say that, Aunt Max?"
"You guys have each other, I don't have anybody in my life," she replies.

M1sh_k@ yells,

M1sh_k@: Liar! Please don't listen to her, Dakshi. She's just using you. Don't listen to her!

I wanted to ask the virtual Mrs. Yang why she harbors hatred towards Ms. Chiu, but it's a deep wound I don't want to touch. As much I want to approach her, I think the best course of action is to give her the space she needs.

Dakshi hugs Ms. Chiu, "Thank you for always being there for me, Aunt Max. I wish my parents understood me as you do."

"Your parents love you very much, Dakshi. Please give them the credit they deserve. You're a good person because of them."

"But I'm crushing the fundraising game at school because of you, Aunt Max. It's definitely not because of my parents. Why couldn't they just sell when they had the chance?" Dakshi whines.

"I wish I could answer that, Dakshi," sighs heavily, "but, you know, Aaron is having a tough time adjusting to Mishka's disappearance. I'm sure you miss her as well."

"I don't know, Aunt Max. My mom was too busy to see the real me. I bet you she doesn't know what my passion in life is."

Ms. Chiu replies, "Be a travel vlogger."

M1sh_k@ covers Ms. Chiu's mouth.

M1sh_k@: Nope. You're wrong, Max. It's building a business from scratch.

Dakshi giggles, "You know me so well, Aunt Max."

M1sh_k@ brings her head down, defeated. She plops herself on the floor and sobs uncontrollably.

I sit next to her and drape my arm around her shoulder. I pull my phone and notice that the digital timer reads: "20:15".

I whisper,

A1d@n: Sorry, Mrs. Yang. We have to go.

Loud banging on the door. Trez opens it. Zen kicks the door close.

She points the pepper spray at Trez and Karen, "You and you," gestures to the sofa, "sit, now!"

Trez and Karen keep their hands up and sit.

"Put the pepper spray down, Zen," begs Karen.

Trez shakes his head, "What's goin' on with ya, Zen? Is it that time of..."

Zen points the pepper spray at Trez, "Shut up, Trez!"

Trez wags his finger at Zen, "You 'bout to get reassigned fo yo dumb actions, ya know?"

Zen points the pepper spray at Trez's eyes, "Who you callin' dumb, huh?!"

Karen shivers, "No, no, no, Zen. Please don't spray him. We're not really together, together. We're just going by the script. Just following orders."

"I don't believe you!" yells Zen as she points the pepper spray at Karen.

"I'm not lying, Zen. Please don't spray me," pleads Karen.

"Go ahead and spray her, Zen. I dare ya," exclaims Trez.

Zen yells, "Don't you dare, dare me, Trez! I'm gonna do it for real."

Trez exhales, "This charade has got to stop, ya hear me?" He swipes the pepper spray from Zen and hands it Karen.

Zen hugs Trez, "I'm sorry, babe. My insecurities got the best of me."

He rubs Zen's back, "Yo, I'm flattered, and all, but yo actions gonna have consequences, ya know what I mean?"

Zen swallows hard, "I know. I'm fully aware."

Karen gets up and hugs Zen, "We're just terrific actors, aren't we Zen?"

"So, you're not pregnant?" asks Zen.

Karen smiles at Zen, "Nah, girl. Of course not. MI6 wouldn't allow it."

Trez clears his throat, "I sleep on the sofa, so that you know, Zen."

Zen hugs Karen, "When did you find out about Trez and me?"

"I've always known. I noticed how distraught you were since I decided to move with him."

Laira's virtual mom, *L@_r1ssa*, and I stand an arm's length away from them.

L@_r1ssa: I don't get it, Aidan. Where's Laira?
A1d@n: I dunno, Mrs. S. Maybe Karen hacked Laira's Prompt account.

Trez sits at the edge of the sofa and gestures to the ladies to do the same. Zen sits in between Trez and Karen.

"I deserved the Metaverse Enforcer assignment, not Dan. I'm a better programmer. He should be the one babysitting," Zen proclaims.

L@_r1ssa taps my shoulder,

L@_r1ssa: What the heck is your mother talking about?
A1d@n shoots L@_r1ssa a death stare.
A1d@n: Don't play dumb, Mrs. S. What is going on?
L@_r1ssa avoids eye contact.
L@_r1ssa: I think it's better if you hear it from your mom...I mean, from Zen.

"I tailed you a few times, but you went missing Zen. Have you been secretly meeting with Vayn?" asks Trez.

Zen nods, "Yep, I've been meeting with Vayn, and he's happy with my contributions. He promised me a promotion. I don't have to babysit anymore. Thank god."

"When are you going to tell Aidan the truth?" asks Karen.

L@_r1ssa shoots me a reassuring look.

L@_r1ssa: I think now's a good time, right, Aidan?

I roll my eyes at the virtual Mrs. S.
Zen pops up, "Follow me to the apartment."
The trio exit the apartment, and virtual Mrs. S and I walk behind them.

◆ ◆ ◆

All of us enter my apartment. Zen closes the entry door. She pulls her phone out and taps on the "VRM3" app, clicking on my "Chat Now" request to *Magic@l_1*.
Zen says, "Hi, Aidan. Hi, Larissa."
Trez and Karen's eyes are about to pop out of its sockets. Zen grins from ear to ear.
Karen approaches me and touches my holographic, virtual self.

L@_r1ssa taps me and whispers,

L@_r1ssa: I think they can see us, Aidan.

"You don't have to whisper, Larissa. We can all hear you," says Zen.
It blows my mind that I've only been using VRM3 for less than an hour, and my mother fixed the so-called glitch that my father was supposed to fix.

A1d@n: How were you able to do that so fast, mom?

Zen approaches me, "Aren't you glad I fixed it faster than Dan did, Aidan? Besides the holographic glitch, I fixed the time-delay issue. So, whenever someone utilizes VRM3, everything will be in real-time. Also, I would like you to know that Dan and I are not your real parents. We were assigned to help you find your way in this world."

A1d@n: I don't get it. What are you talking about?

I approach Karen and inquire,

A1d@n: What is she talking about, Karen?

Karen and I lock eyes, "I think you should sit, Aidan."
Despite being in a virtual space, my mind and my heart is dumbfounded and conflicted.
I run to my room, and I see the real me with a VRM3 headset on. I notice tears trickling down my cheeks.
I think to myself, "There's another side to this story. I have to hear Dan's side."
I pick-up my phone and close out my group "Chat Now" with *Magic@l_1* and *L@_r1ssa*. I also close my group "Chat Now" with *B1t_n@*, *Y@_yo1*, *M1sh_k@*, and *L@_r1ssa*.

My virtual self and *D@_1ien* lock eyes as we stand on the rooftop of my school.

D@_1ien: Sorry we kept this a secret for so long, Aidan. We don't mean to hurt your feelings. We were just, you know...

I interrupt his excuse or lie. It doesn't even matter if he's telling the truth. It's too painful to swallow the pill right now.

A1d@n: playing the part, I know. I got the gist from Zen and Karen. Are you even a real Brit?

D@_1ien lets loose a nervous chuckle.

D@_1ien: I am, indeed, Aidan. I am a programmer for MI6's Internet Security Division, otherwise known as MIF or Monarchy's Internet Force. Karen is my wife in real life.
A1d@n: Is she a real American?
D@_1ien: Yes, she is, born in Reno, Nevada, but grew up in NorCal.
A1d@n: What about Zen?
D@_1ien: Zen works for the CIA, Central Internet Agency, and is romantically involved with Trez.
A1d@n: Were you really missing?
D@_1ien: Yes, and no. Yes, because I failed to fix Verme's time-delay issue. My consciousness misled me to believe that I have been gone for a month. No, because we lived in a secret facility.
A1d@n: What is up with the secrecy?
D@_1ien: The four moms weren't getting along with their partnered actors, and Vayn noticed that it's not healthy for the kids. Henceforth, we agreed to spin the narrative that we went missing.
A1d@n: Oh, I see. What about the missing four moms?
D@_1ien: They're all actors. Come to think of it, we all were.
A1d@n: I still don't get it. Are you saying Earl, Jair, Dakshi, and Laira are orphans, too?
D@_1ien: Check your phone and see what time it is.

I pull my phone out, and the digital timer reads: "00:15".

A1d@n: It's not fair. I don't wanna go. I want to stay here. I hate the real world.

T he room's layout is similar to SCT's school principal office. However, the framed certificates (Ph.D. in Psychology, Ph.D. in Neuroscience, MBA in Computer Science, Economics & Business Administration, Bachelor's degree in Computer Science, Business Administration, Economics & Physics) from prestigious universities are for Dr. Vayn Reale.

Earlier in the story, the VR guy in a drone-like helicopter now wears a white lab coat with his name embroidered in a blue thread, a grey polo shirt, blue jeans, and colorful sneakers. He is the real Dr. Vayn Reale.

He sits next to Aidan, and across from him is Zen Peet.

Aidan wears headphones and holds her phone close to her face as she intently watches an animated show.

Zen covers her face with her palm as she sobs uncontrollably.

The VRM3 goggles and a laptop rests on the desk. The image on the computer is a tall glass building similar to Aidan's virtual world.

Dr. Reale grabs a tissue box from his desk and hands it to Zen, "Here you go, Mrs. Peet."

Zen mouths, "Thank you," and grabs a handful of tissues and wipes her tears.

Dr. Reale utters, "Aidan is a wonderful storyteller, Mrs. Peet. She's able to fictionalize her feelings through an elaborate Sci-Fi-like story. I'm really proud of her."

Zen clears her throat, "Not to sound like negative Nancy, doctor. But why does my character appear like I'm the villain in the story when, in fact, my husband left me to be the sole caregiver?"

He replies, "Please don't look at it that way, Mrs. Peet. We have only seen the beginning of Aidan's complex story. And we'll allow Aidan to explain her story to us."

Zen sighs heavily and inquires, "How is she able to craft a complex story like that when she's a low-functioning nonverbal teen with Autism and Intellectual Disability?"

He smiles, "Oh, Mrs. Peet, your daughter is super smart. Indeed, she's not able to communicate her thought and feelings through speech or even written form," gestures to the VRM3 goggles, "but through this technological breakthrough, she's able to convey to us what's in her heart."

Aidan hands her headphones and phone to her mom.

Zen grabs a tablet from her bag. She taps on an app called "TouchChat" (AAC - Augmentative & Alternative Communication) and gives it to Aidan.

Zen asks, "All done with the phone, Aidan?"

Aidan repeatedly blinks, rocks her body while she holds her AAC device, taps the words "All done," then taps, "Thank you."

Dr. Reale says, "Beautiful story, Aidan," adds, "I'm going to ask you some questions about your story, is that okay, Aidan?"

Aidan taps, "Yes."

He asks, "Were you listening to the Drake rap song in the cafeteria and singing along, Aidan?"

Aidan taps, "Yes."

"Did the kids laugh at you?"

Aidan taps her response, "Yes."

"Is Karen your ABA behaviorist?"

Aidan taps, "Yes."

"Is Michel your Speech therapist?"

Aidan taps, "Yes."

"How about Earl, Jair, Dakshi, and Laira, are they your classmates?"

Aidan taps, "No."

"Did they make fun of you?"

Aidan taps, "No."

Dr. Reale looks at Zen.

"Are those the cool kids at South City Tech?"

Aidan taps, "Yes."

Dr. Reale smiles at Zen.

"You know what, Aidan, when I was in high school, I wasn't cool like those kids, too, you know. Do you think it would be nice to be cool like them?"

Aidan taps, "Yes."

"Did you fictionalize the cool kids with their mom's missing as well?"

Aidan taps, "Yes."

"So, your story is very cool; did the movie Sixth Sense inspire you?"

Aidan taps, "Yes."

Zen caresses Aidan's knees.

"What do you feel when you don't get to do what you want to do?"

Aidan taps her response, "Frustrated."

"Did you play Pokemon Go before?"

Aidan taps, "Yes."

"Did you play that with your dad?"

Aidan taps, "Yes."

"Do you see yourself as a ghost in your story because people in real life ignore you?"

Aidan taps, "Yes."

Aidan rocks her body intensely, grunts, distressed. She taps, "Yes."

"Do you miss your dad, Aidan?"

Zen interrupts, exclaims, "Doctor, please!"

Aidan grunts louder and taps, "Yes," and then taps "Frustrated."

Zen hugs Aidan tightly, comforting her.

"I'm sorry, Zen. Sorry, Aidan. I think that's it for now," Dr. Reale ruffles Aidan's hair, "wonderful session, Aidan. I hope to see more of your stories next session, okay? I can't wait."

Aidan taps, "Thank you," and an icon with Dr. Reale's image, "Doctor Reale."

END OF EPISODE 1

ABOUT THE AUTHOR

Dexter Alvaro

Dexter Alvaro is a family man who loves reading Mystery, Science Fiction, Thriller & YA books. He channels his characters by listening to music. He loves watching sports, bingeing TV series, documentary films & series, reading economics-related books & listening to podcasts.

Medium: https://dexteralvaro.medium.com
Instagram: https://instagram.com/dex_alvaro